north east

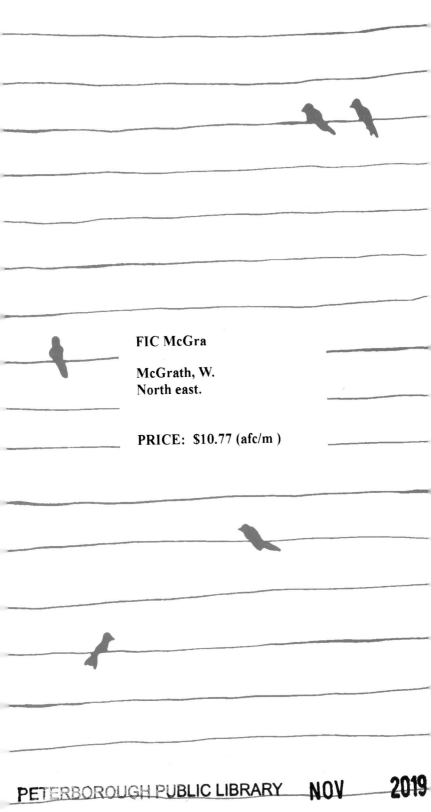

FIC McGra

McGrath, W.
North east.

PRICE: $10.77 (afc/m )

Wendy McGrath

*a novel*

# NORTH

# EAST

NeWest Press

Copyright Wendy McGrath 2014

North East is available as an ebook: 978-1-927063-73-6

*Library and Archives Canada Cataloguing in Publication*
McGrath, Wendy, author
North east / Wendy McGrath.

Issued in print and electronic formats.
ISBN 978-1-927063-72-9 (pbk.). – ISBN 978-1-927063-73-6 (epub). –
ISBN 978-1-927063-74-3 (mobi)

I. Title.

PS8575.G74N67 2014     C813'.6     C2014-901647-6
                                   C2014-901648-4

Editor: Douglas Barbour
Book design: Natalie Olsen, Kisscut Design
Cover photo: Toby Dickens
Author photo: Kylie Kennedy

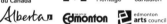

NeWest Press acknowledges the support of the Canada Council
for the Arts, the Alberta Foundation for the Arts, and the
Edmonton Arts Council for support of our publishing program.
We acknowledge the financial support of the Government of Canada
through the Canada Book Fund for our publishing activities.

#201, 8540 – 109 Street
Edmonton, AB T6G 1E6
780.432.9427
NeWest Press    www.newestpress.com

*No bison were harmed in the making of this book.*

Printed and bound in Canada

*For my Mother,*
*with love and gratitude*

I think, that if I touched the earth,
  It would crumble;
It is so sad and beautiful,
So tremulously like a dream.


DYLAN THOMAS, "Clown in the Moon"

prologue

The basement in October.


Her mother lifted the ring in the door that was cut
into the floor of the kitchen. The door opened to a dirt
basement where she did the laundry with a wringer
washing machine. Christine imagined the door led to
a secret passage, a way to some magical place.


The only light that shone down there was the band
of light from the kitchen. Illuminating the flimsy
stairs, which were more like a ladder, leading straight
down into the earth. Her mother descended into this
place of dirt walls a wringer washing machine with a
framework of shelves to hold the jars of canning she
had put up. The smooth cold glass the thick silver lids
tightened tightened tight.


Sometimes Christine was allowed to come down the
stairs with her mother. The sound of water as the
machine churned the clothes we were swimmers in
the lake the smell of earth the dirt walls steam rising
from the belly of the machine and there was the light
on the rows of jars filled with colour with the red of

raspberry jam with the blue-purple of chokecherry jelly
the soft pink of crabapple jelly the complexity of relish.
Surrounded by colour by earth by water by the smell
of soap the taste of the colour the sweet taste of
raspberries chokecherries. She inhaled and held her
breath. Living in a secret painting underground
undersea. The taste of colour the taste of red and
pink and purple. She is happy. This day is full of colour
and she can taste it on her tongue the sunlight red and
yellow and orange so happy she is afraid to say anything.
She doesn't want to open her mouth she wants to
keep the taste of these colours on her tongue and this
happiness inside her. She wants to keep this moment
with the sun shining and her mother in the basement
humming and the noise of the washing machine and
the smell of earth and soap. She wants to be able to
keep this moment forever somehow so the happiness
can't get away from her and disappear the way it
seemed to in this house.

I

The sun was shining when the girl opened her eyes that morning, but the house was quiet. Usually when she woke there were those soft noises in the house that made her happy and let her know everything was alright. Even if her father had already gone to work, her mother would be out in the kitchen. The radio would make its music, there would be the quiet rattle of dishes hitting against each other in the sink, the floor squeaking under her mother's footsteps. The girl would smell coffee boiling in the glass pot on the stove. But, this morning, when she opened her eyes there was none of that. The sunlight through the window escaped from the edges of the curtains onto the wall. She hadn't noticed this before, but now it made her feel that there was something to be afraid of. She listened hard. Outside she could only hear the sounds of birds and traffic and the barking of the neighbours' dog, Tatters. Inside, all she could hear was her heart beating. Still the sun shone.

Slowly, quietly, she pulled back the covers and pulled her nightie down over her knees. She walked quietly from her bed to bedroom door. The door to her parents' room was closed. She turned down the hall toward the kitchen touching the cool white wall as she

quietly made her way. It was summer but she thought
of that Christmas poem: "Not a creature was stirring. . ."
The wall was cold and her fingers felt the small bumps
on the plaster. The light in the hall was yellow and blue
and pink all at once and she could taste the colours as
she stood at the door of the kitchen.

There was her father, standing at the counter by himself.
Why wasn't he working today? She watched him jab an
old spoon into a big tin full of light brown powder. The
tin had a muscle man on the front. She walked quietly
toward her father as he scooped the powder from the
tin into a stained old MELMAC bowl, holding it under
the kitchen faucet where only a trickle of water escaped.
She was standing behind her father now and watched
him stir the water into the powder a bit at a time until
it looked like the cookie dough her mother made.
– What's that Dad?

He jumped, but, when he turned to her, with a cigarette
between his lips, he looked like himself.

The cigarette moved when he talked.
– Putty.
– What for?
– Just fixing a little nick in the cupboard.
– How'd it get there?

Her father stopped stirring the putty, pinched the cigarette between his thumb and index finger, and took a deep puff. Christine heard the cigarette crackle and saw the tip turn bright red. He balanced the cigarette on the edge of counter with the tip facing out, and then laughed.

– I was practicing a knife trick.

– Did Mom get mad at you?

– Oh ya. She told me I'd better fix that P D Q.

The girl laughed like she always did when her father said P D Q because it meant Pretty Darn Quick and she thought the sound of those words together was funny. She saw those letters in her mind P D Q. As she watched her father smooth the brown putty into the groove on the cupboard door she heard the birds outside again and the scrape of the putty knife as her father smoothed the mud over the nick.

– Can you show me the trick Dad?

– No. I told your Mom I'd only do that trick once.

– Can you show me that trick?

He had bent over so his face was right by hers and he held the bowl with the putty in one hand and the putty knife in the other.

– *Never* touch those knives in the drawer. Understand?

She was quiet.

– Understand? *Do you understand?*

She didn't know what she'd done or said to make her father so angry, she didn't know what to do or where to move. She could smell the putty and it made her think of crayons or paint. She looked toward the knives in the drawer now that her father had said she couldn't touch them, imagining what they would feel like, what they could do. She had seen them all laid out on the kitchen table before, when a man had come to sharpen them for her mother. He had lined up the knives on a piece of grey felt and now, as she pictured them, she tasted sharp metal on her tongue.

– Yes.


What was the knife trick? Why did her father get so mad? She hadn't touched the knives and she hadn't cut herself with them. She was afraid of her father and stood in the middle of the kitchen watching him smooth the putty on the cupboard door. The birds outside, the quiet of the house, her parents' bedroom door opening and then, her mother in the kitchen, pink housecoat, pale blue nightie, and a piece of dangling lace from its hem, ripped and brushing the top of her foot. It made Christine sad to see this tattered piece of lace. The piece of lace stopped just above a tiny cut on her mother's foot.

– Finally up?
– I heard you. I just didn't want to talk to you.
  Didn't want to look at you.
– Don't then.
– Did your Dad get you something to eat, Christine?

- No.
- She's been helping me. Right, Christine?

The girl was in the middle of the kitchen between her mother and father.
- She doesn't need to help you. Don't try to. . .your Dad doesn't need your help.

When she looked at Christine, it was as if her mother suddenly did wake up. She straightened, walked back to the bedroom and came back to the kitchen with her pink slippers clapping with the floor.
- Rice Krispies? Corn flakes?
- Corn flakes.
- Please?
- Please.

Her mother walked past her father as if he were invisible, opened the cupboard door, reached for the cereal box and then slammed the door shut. Christine's father picked up his cigarette from the edge of the cupboard. It had gotten short and ashes fell to the floor. He stayed at the counter, not looking at her mother, but just smoking his cigarette. Neither of her parents looked at the other. When Christine's mother shook cereal into her bowl, she saw the piece of lace still hanging down from her nightie, but her slippers covered the cut on her foot. It had disappeared and was gone, just like the nick in the cupboard.

- What happened to your foot Mom?
- What d'you mean?
- I saw a cut on your foot. What happened?
- Nothing. Never mind and eat your breakfast.

Her mother slid her feet under her chair. Christine ate her cornflakes and thought about the putty her father had made, how it was so good to use to fix something and hide something. A mistake.

By the time her father had filled the nick with putty and touched up the paint, the door looked the same as before. No one would ever know he had hit the cupboard doing a knife trick. He had made the putty turn into a part of the cupboard door. Christine thought maybe she could make things out of putty too. She could mix it and make it into things she imagined, those pictures or feelings or colours that came to her mind or that she would sometimes taste on her tongue. She could use the putty to make those things into something real.
- Good as new.

The door squeaked when her father opened it and shut it.
- You're welcome he said to Christine's mother.
- What?
- For making the cupboard look so damn nice again and he laughed.

– I sure as hell won't thank you. . .
– Don't forget, I'm full of tricks and he laughed again.
  Wanna go for a drive Christine?
– She's not going anywhere. She's eating her
  breakfast.
– I can hurry. I want to go. She scooped the corn
  flakes into her mouth quickly now.
– No, slow down. You just stay here.
– But I want to go with Dad.
– You're not going anywhere with him.

Her father looked at her mother without saying
a word, he just smiled. Christine's mother wasn't
smiling. She looked angry, but there was something
else. Christine thought her mother seemed scared,
but was trying to pretend she wasn't and she didn't
know what exactly her father would be smiling about,
there was nothing funny. He put the putty, stained
MELMAC bowl, and putty knife under the kitchen
sink and then stood for a second looking at the nick
in the cupboard. Then he turned quickly toward the
porch and pounded his feet into his work boots, not
bothering to lace them, and was out the back door
without saying a word. Christine ran to the window
to wave to him and, as he backed out of the driveway,
he was still smiling to himself in that strange way.
She waved as hard as she could, but he didn't see her.

⟨⟩⟨⟩⟨⟩

Christine thought about her father's knife trick and the putty her father had used to fix the cupboard door. When she was in the kitchen, she would look for the spot and remember her father's warning. She never talked about the knife trick after that day. But she thought about the knives in the drawer and what it would be like to touch them.

She was thinking about the tin with the muscle man under the sink, the knife trick, and the knives on this day when her mother was in the cellar doing laundry. Christine hadn't asked to go down there with her as she usually did. She stayed in the kitchen listening to the swoosh swoosh of the wringer washing machine and peeked over the opening in the floor to see that her mother was still taking clothes out of the tub and feeding them through the rollers. Usually, she loved to watch the thick pieces of laundry feed through the rollers and slither out the other side flat and into the metal pail but, today, she could only think about the sharp silver knives in the drawer.

She took the tin of putty powder, the MELMAC bowl and the putty knife from under the sink and put it on the counter. Quietly she slid a kitchen chair over to the sink and mixed the putty the way she had seen her father do, adding drops of water as she mixed it with the powder to the brrrr and hum of the washing machine rollers.

She spooned some putty into her palm and rolled it between her hands into a smooth ball and then flattened it like the clothes and towels squeezed through the wringers of the washing machine in the basement. She peeled the putty from her hand and began rolling it again. She shaped it again into a smooth ball thinking about how the putty could be so many things and she could make it into shapes that could maybe tell a story or keep a secret. She flattened the ball of putty in the palm of her hand and it smelled like the basement and the nick in the cupboard and she tasted metal and earth. She almost lost her balance as she stepped off the chair still holding the disk of putty in her palm. Still holding the disk, she opened the door where the cutlery, and the sharp knives, were kept and reached for the handle of one the man had sharpened, even though she knew she wasn't supposed to touch those. She used the tip of the knife to make a mark in the disk, like the one her father had made in the cupboard door with his trick.

Making this mark, she felt as if she was doing a special trick, like her father, and she would keep this disk a secret, like her father kept his trick a secret. This mark, in this disk, made her remember her father's trick with the knife, her mother's face that morning in the kitchen, the small cut on her mother's foot, and her father driving away pretending he didn't see Christine waving at the window. This disk showed she remembered what happened that day but she hid it at the back of the closet in her bedroom so her mother and father wouldn't know she still remembered, so they would think she had forgotten.

II

The girl had taken the curved white feather from under a hen when she and her grandmother went to collect the eggs. The chicken coop was faded grey and the windows were dirty. The chickens were waking up and they were making some noise inside. Her grandmother carried a bucket of chicken feed and she wore rubber boots because the ground was still wet. The girl clomped along in the see-through boots with a big button on the side and a brown elastic ring around it that made the boot tops tight but, even then, they were still too big for the girl. Her grandmother wore these boots for 'good' when she went into town or to church if it was raining and muddy. They fit over her high heels and they were the only boots that came close to fitting her grand-daughter. The girl felt so beautiful wearing those big boots. The chicken coop had a door that her grandmother pulled down like a drawbridge on a castle. When it touched the ground her grandmother started making clucking noises and scattered the feed around the outside of the faded old chicken coop. The chickens came running down the drawbridge of the chicken coop so many of them out of such a small place. Her grandmother was like a magician opening a secret door and all those funny birds came out. She followed her grandmother inside the chicken coop. The chickens had laid some eggs and when she picked them up they were warm. Her grandmother held her apron to make a pouch

and the girl gently laid them in. Some of the shells were
brown and some were spotted and some looked like they
had dirt on them. But they were so beautiful all piled in
her grandmother's apron and she thought how glad she
was to have her grandmother because if her grandmother
was queen of the chicken coop castle then she was the
princess. The girl plucked a white feather from the straw
and put it in the pocket of her corduroy pants.

Back home she thought of the disk she had made and
hidden in the back of her closet. She would make
another. She waited until her father had gone to work.
Her mother was up and making the bed. The girl heard
the scrape of the bed's wheels on the floor. Then she
heard her mother's footsteps on the floor as she walked
to the bathroom. The door shut. The girl heard the
water running in the bathroom sink and knew she had
to hurry. She got out the tin of putty with the muscle
builder on it and thought how much he reminded her of
Popeye. Oh how she loved that cartoon. She felt strong
this morning too and imagined she was in a cartoon
and she watched herself as she popped the silver lid
off with a big spoon and it flipped onto the floor and
made a clinking sound. She quickly picked it up spilling
some of the powder on the floor in front of the sink.
It looked like the dust that puffed out from under her
bare feet on those hot summer days when she ran outside
her grandmother's house on the farm. She brushed
the powder with her free hand until it just seemed to

*become part of the floor. As she quickly spooned some of the powder into the blue M E L M A C bowl from under the sink she heard the toilet flush. Quickly she took a kitchen chair to the sink and held the bowl under the tap letting the water dribble into the powder. Mixing. More water and now mixing again and as she stirred she thought of her grandmother and something magic and the chickens and the chicken coop and the putty smelled like each of those things and all of them at once. She thought of the yellow straw and the warm eggs in her grandmother's apron. To the girl, the putty smelled of the air and the ground at her grandmother's farm and the trees and that morning with her grandmother and the chickens. She stirred the mixture with a fork put the bowl on the kitchen counter and moved the chair back under the table. She scraped the putty out of the bowl and put it into the palm of her left hand cradling the soft mound. With her free hand she put the bowl under the sink and shut the door. Quickly quickly she molded the putty into a soft disk and then she took the feather and pressed it into the putty rocking her fingers over it back and forth. This impression on the surface of the putty looked like fine cracks in the shell of an egg, small wrinkles in the clothes of a queen, the fine light feather threads of luck and beauty.*

*The girl slipped past the bathroom door just as her mother opened it and ran to her room hiding this disk in the dark at the back of her closet.*

She stared at her mother's hat resting so quiet and rich on the top shelf of her parents' closet. It had a soft brown velvet brim and white feathers curved around the crown. The tips of some of the feathers were peeking out brown with white dots and that hat was amazing because it stayed so solid and fixed to the shelf and yet the girl thought the feathers made it seem as if it could just fly away when she wasn't looking and if it really wanted to. Anyway, maybe the hat had thoughts of its own or it could absorb all the thoughts and made-up stories of the person who wore the hat and keep them under the velvet brim and hide them in between the soft feathers as if they were eggs and keep them warm until they escaped.

What did her Mother think about when she wore that hat? Did she daydream and make things up or draw things in her mind like the girl did or think of a picture that she could hold in her hand or keep in a pocket or under that hat? She imagined her mother didn't take these daydreams out to look at much just like some of the hats and clothes her mother seldom wore and kept for good. There were a few beautiful things that the girl hardly ever saw her mother wear.

But she remembered her mother had worn that hat
to her uncle's wedding. Her mother wore a bright red
jacket and skirt and brown high-heel shoes. And she
had posed for the picture the girl had seen in a photo
album. Her mother was there with the whole family
except the bride because she was from a different family
and it was before the wedding and so the bride wasn't
allowed to see the groom. There they were all outside
the girl's grandmother's house because they had moved
from the farm to town and they were standing under
the clothesline with sheets flapping. No one looked
up. No one paid attention to all the clothes on the line
flapping in the wind. No one seemed to hear the noise
of the clothes clicking and cracking in the wind. The
feathers on her mother's hat flipped up and down in
the wind too. Her mother and her aunt and her other
uncles and her grandparents stood in their best clothes
under the flapping white sheets. Maybe it sounded like
clapping and maybe the clothes were clapping for all
of them in their good clothes and their hats and their
shiny shoes. The girl's grandmother's hat was brown
and it had the eye of a peacock feather tucked into the
smooth brown ribbon that circled the crown and she
was wearing a brown dress and she had put on red
lipstick and she was so beautiful she didn't look like the
same grandmother-on-the-farm the girl came to visit
in Saskatchewan and she couldn't remember when her
grandmother-on-the-farm became her grandmother-
who-moved-to-town. And the clothes kept on flapping

in the wind and no one paid attention to the noise and this made the girl feel sad. All the people in this picture were married or going to be married and even though they were laughing and wearing their best clothes she felt they weren't really happy.

Her mother's hat could tell those stories without even using words and the girl would just feel them in her mind and on her skin like those feathers so soft and light. She wished she could turn herself into that hat for half-an-hour and she knew how long that was now. One episode of Batman or the Monkees. She would be that hat with no commercials for a half-an-hour and then turn back into her old self. If she were the hat she would be able to feel what her Mother felt and think what her Mother thought and she believed this could happen.

– Are you and Dad happy Mom?
– Of course. Don't worry about those kinds of things.
– You don't seem happy she said and the girl thought of the hockey pants her father still had in the back of the closet and his skates that he never used she thought of the pretty shoes in her mother's closet that she couldn't remember her wearing and the sparkly earrings she had in the blue velvet case in her drawer and she never wore those either. Then she started to cry.
– What? Why are you crying? What is it?

And the girl's father came into her parents' bedroom and he asked her what was wrong and she said she was sad because she wished it could be that time when they were happy and she thought they weren't because they never laughed or smiled and her father asked if she wanted to go to tastee-freez for a nut dip ice cream and she stopped crying and said she was already in her pyjamas but her father told her nobody would care and they'd just go.

She tucked her pyjama bottoms into her long white socks and put on her rubber boots and her white sweater. Probably nobody would be able to tell she was in her pyjamas.

In the front seat of the car with her father and the blue lights from dash shone out toward them and when her father turned the car down 118th avenue the streetlights shone yellow and he was smoking his cigarette and the end was bright red and the girl straightened her legs and her pyjamas peeked out from under her coat a little bit. Her eyes burned because of her tears but the cool air felt good on her face. She was feeling happy again now the radio played that song by Petula Clark she liked so much about going downtown with bright lights and not being lonely. They weren't going downtown but as they drove along 118th avenue there were streetlights shining over them with their bright heads on their long necks and the star on the circle sign in front of the gas station with the two lights shining above that star and then she saw the blue tastee-freez sign and it was happy too and pretty with its bright white letters and ice cream cone. The ice cream sat on top of the gold cone just like the feathers sat on top of her mother's hat.

This made her think of the fairy tale her mother read to her about a girl who had six brothers who had all been turned into swans and their sister had to be quiet and say nothing for six years for the spell to be broken. And there was more. Not only did the sister have to be quiet for six years she had to make each one of her brothers a shirt out of flowers so they could put them on and turn back into people forever. She almost did it. The sister in the fairy tale didn't speak for such a long time and she threw the shirts over the swans who were really her brothers but she just didn't have enough time to finish a sleeve on one of the shirts so it couldn't cover a brother's wing and so he had a wing instead of an arm. Forever and ever in the story.

The girl was wearing her favourite white sweater with red buttons over her pyjamas. If she had one wing it would be hard to get through the arm of her sweater and how would she do up the buttons if she only had one hand and one arm? She would have to ask someone to help her. That was all there was to it. She thought of the seagulls she would see looking out the window when they drove out of the city past the dump. Seagulls flying and fighting over some bit of food and she knew they could never be as beautiful as swans no matter how hard they tried. They made a terrible sound. And why were they called seagulls? They didn't live near the sea they lived in garbage so their name didn't even make sense. She would never make flower shirts for those birds even if they were related to her and she would never keep quiet for six years for them or for anybody. White swans with white feathers and her white sweater and white ice cream in the cone on the tastee-freez sign. The lights were bright like in the song and she felt happy and hoped her parents were never sad again.

Her father parked the car beside the tastee-freez and she stood on tip-toe at the window when she ordered a special nut-dip cone in her pyjamas under her sweater and rubber boots and no one even cared. When she reached for the cone she imagined her arm was the wing of a swan and she took her time wrapping her fingers slowly around the cone as the woman handed it to her. Her fingers were long white wing feathers wrapping around the cone like it was a queen's scepter and the nuts were precious jewels.

- Hurry, take the cone Christine.
- Dad what if I had one wing and one hand?
- What? Well "You can't fly home on one wing". . . that's what my gramma would say to us when we came to see her.
- What did that mean Dad?
- If you said it was time to go she would say that and pour you another drink.
- Even kids?
- Well for the kids it was this poppy tea.
- Tea made from flowers? and the girl crunched the salty nuts and the ice cream melted around them in her mouth. Her father laughed.
- A special kind of flower. . .a special kind of poppy my gramma grew and she kept the seeds for tea. If we were getting rambunctious she would make us this tea and it would make us really sleepy and quiet. She also used to say "Children should be seen and not heard."
- She sounds mean! Is she still alive?
- No, she died when I was little.
- Did she ever give you ice cream cones or get you a nut-dip at the tastee-freez?
- There were no tastee-freez when I was a kid.
- I'm glad I'm alive in these times she said and licked some of the ice cream as it melted.
- Me too.

She loved her father at this moment while he was eating his chocolate dip cone and she thought he was happy now. He seemed happy when she looked at him because nothing was in black and white like the pictures at home in the drawers. Everything was in colour and if she had a camera she would take a picture of him now with the blue yellow gold colours of the tastee-freez shining all around him.

The picture she would take would be different from those black and white pictures her mother kept in the bottom drawer of the "chiffonier" in her parents' bedroom. The word "chiffonier" made the girl think of a woman talking on the phone but she could not think what that had to do with this piece of furniture, the drawers, or the photographs but it made sense to her because she also thought that the word "engagement" had something to do with riding elevators and when she thought of her mother wearing the feather hat at her uncle's wedding she imagined her aunt and uncle getting into an elevator and the doors closing on them. Did those same doors close for her mother and father when they were engaged and got on an elevator?

– I don't want you to die Dad. I don't want Mom to die either. And I don't want to die.

– What made you think of that? C'mon kids shouldn't be thinking about those kinds of things.

The girl felt like she was going to start crying again.

– I don't know how to stop thinking about these
   kinds of things. They just come into my head and
   I can't stop them.

There were loose, black and white pictures of her
parents layered on the bottom of a special drawer and
pictures in envelopes and big books with more photos
in them. The books were thick and heavy and one had
a picture of mountains, and trees and a lake where a
white deer was in the water and its neck was bowing
to drink the blue water. Some of the pictures were of
her mother and father when they were younger and
it was before she was born and they were teenagers
and her mother wore lipstick and her father wore a big
dressy coat and nice shoes and his hair was like Elvis
Presley's. They seemed to love each other. They were
younger and happy. Once when she was looking at the
old pictures the girl felt old herself thinking of how
long ago it must be. So the girl thought she must be
old now too. She felt old. But when she looked in
the mirror there were no wrinkles and no grey hair.
She was still only five.

– Those pictures are funny. Your Mom and I were
   having fun with our friends. Things change. C'mon
   you're just a little kid and these are the good times
   of life. You should be happy. You have nothing to
   worry about.

Now looking at her father and eating her ice cream cone at the wood table outside the tastee-freez she was feeling happy again.

– Dad I hope you'll never die and Mom will never die and I'll never die.

– Let's not talk about this now. Are you finished your cone?

– I don't know if I can finish all this Dad.

– It's okay, you don't have to eat it all. He took the soggy cone from her hand and threw it on the small patch of grass in front of the tastee-freez. Gulls swooped down to it flapping and screeching the yellow from the streetlight and the white from the tastee-freez sign making their beaks and their wings seem much bigger in their shadows.

– I'm thirsty now.

– Okay let's get a pop.

She held her father's hand and didn't look at the birds as they walked back to the window and she thought this must be the best night ever. It was late and she was out with her Dad and they both had their favourite cones and they were both happy now.

– Cream soda please. What do you want Christine?

– Cream soda please. She wanted to ask for the same thing as her father and like what he liked.

She felt sorry for him because his gramma had made him drink flower tea.

They walked back to the table and the girl drank from a striped straw that got soggy after a little while and her father finished his pop and lit a cigarette and just looked out to the road with the cars going back and forth.

– Dad, don't worry. I told you we're never going to die.
– What? and he looked at her as if he just woke up. What?
– We're not going to die.
– Sweetheart, everybody dies.
– C'mon Dad let's go home now. I'm finished.


In the car on the way home she thought about what her father had said and didn't want to believe him. When she got home she hugged her mother.

– Feeling better now?
– I'm not as sad.
– Good. Now it's past your bedtime so scoot and brush your teeth.
– Come with me?
– Okay, this time. Her mother was being nice to her because of the crying before.
– In the bathroom the girl put some toothpaste on the brush.
– Mom when will we die?
– No one knows when they're going to die.
– Are we all going to die? Really is that the truth? Dad said.
– Yes, but not for a long, long time.
– But you said we didn't know. . .

- Well, that's why we have to make the most of the time we have. Try not to think about it.
- I can't stop thinking about it now Mom.
- If you hurry we can read a story tonight, what about that?

The girl ran for her bed and her mother pulled back the bedspread and lifted up the covers and it was cold for a little while but her mother lay on the bed beside her and it was warm now.
- How about the story about the six swans and their sister?
- Okay, we haven't read that in a long time.

But the girl fell asleep before they got to the part about the flower-shirts the sister had to make.

That night she dreamt:

A big wall was in front of her and it was thickly painted blue. But she saw it was actually a door and she had covered this big door with a layer of plaster over a layer of wire and sand. When she brought out the key she wanted to open the door but in her dream she was afraid of what was on the other side. She put the key in the lock it began to smoke from the lock that had been covered over and over with thick white paint. She put her hand on the door and pieces of blue plaster began to fall away and she could see the

wires poking through. She tried to pat the pieces of
plaster back into place and to open the door. It was so
heavy and big but when the girl shouted for help no
one came. Then the door opened on its own and the
girl looked out from the big door and was surprised.
There were people half-naked dancing and flipping
and doing cartwheels. People were walking quickly
carrying tables and big sheets of wood. Her father was
behind her.

– Don't put on airs and remember people don't like it
   when you play the fool.

Then she was at her grandmother's house and she
saw two peacock feathers pinned crossed above her
grandmother's bedroom door. Their big blue eyes at
the top looking down at her.

– Peacock feathers mean good luck her grandmother
   said.

The eye was a heart and the feathers were like green
threads and so much shine. Threads of feathers and
feathers of threads. Green and bright blue and gold.
Then she was feeding chickens with her grandmother
and the chickens were coming out of the coop on their
drawbridge, marching and laying eggs that rolled
down the ramp and into the dirt and broke and the
yolks spread and the yellow covered the ground and
the girl and her grandmother tried to run from the
flood of eggs and the egg shells turned to feathers and

blew away and her grandmother shouted at her to go find her mother and father. But in her dream she knew her father was dead and her mother was dead.

She woke up and couldn't breathe. Gasping and coughing she kicked off her covers and the light in her bedroom came on and her parents were at her bedroom door and then standing over her reaching for her.

— Jesus Christ what is it? Christine! Christine!

— Let me help you!

But the girl slapped at them and kicked them away scared she was dying and if her mother or father touched her they might die too. She couldn't catch her breath it was like hands were on her throat choking her tighter and tighter. Coughing and choking her eyes were wide open now and she sat up trying to catch her breath coughing and coughing. Gradually her breath came back and she was awake now and looking at her parents who looked so worried and tried again to come and help her but she pushed them away.

— No leave me alone!

Sitting on the side of the bed she pulled her pyjama bottoms up past her knees. Breathing. Breathing. Things were quieter. There. She could breathe again now. Then she started to cry. Her parents came toward her again and this time she let them get close to her. Her mother put her hand to the girl's forehead.

– What is it? Why wouldn't you let us help you?
– Did you have a nightmare?
– What is it? What is it?
– I was scared. I was afraid.
– What were you scared of?
– I don't know now. I don't remember.

But the girl was lying. She couldn't tell them in her dream they were both dead and now she knew she would die one day.

– C'mon sweetheart let's get you back to sleep.

Her mother and father smoothed her pillow and straightened the sheets and the bedspread and it was nice and cool when it covered her. The light ticked off and her father and mother were standing over her and talking quietly.

– Go to sleep now, okay?
– We'll be right here in the living room so you can call us. We'll be right here.

Christine closed her eyes and drew her knees up under the covers.

III

*The girl put wood putty powder in a blue MELMAC*
*cup. She twisted the tap so just a drizzle of water came*
*out and held the cup underneath. Her mother was*
*sleeping and she didn't know for how long so she*
*stirred it quickly first with a fork then a shiny teaspoon.*
*It looked like the stiff peanut butter cookie dough*
*her mother made but she knew she couldn't eat it.*
*She scooped the putty from the cup and shaped it into*
*a small ball the way she had seen her mother do.*
*Then she took the extra key to the car from her*
*mother's snap-shut purse and pressed it into the putty.*
*The impression looked like a sword or a tree or a jagged*
*mountain but it was their blue car their Galaxie 500.*

*For now, she hid the disk under her bed.*

It was warm and summer was coming through the car's open windows. It was the smell of dry sweet flowers and she knew the birds she saw flying in front of the car were happy and even the birds that she couldn't see were happy hiding in trees or resting in their nests. The girl was so sure of happy that when they passed the big lake she knew all the fish in the water were happy too and even if there were monsters or dinosaurs in that lake they would be so happy that they wouldn't even bother eating the fish and would let them just swim and live.

Christine sat in between her mother and father in the front seat of the Galaxie 500. It wasn't a seat really it was a hard tough blue between her parents and the girl had to make sure her feet didn't hit the gearshift while her father was driving. This part of the front seat was smooth and the same colour as her favourite MELMAC bowl. She imagined she was curled in that same bowl as she sat between her parents making sure her feet didn't get too close to the gearshift. Her spoon always made a high sound that matched the colour of the bowl when she scooped up her puffed wheat or Rice Krispies and when she was left with just the milk it was like a circle-cloud in a round blue sky. The radio made that same tinny sound and she imagined the songs scooping the air and she was breathing in the music and swallowing the words of the songs. *"Blue velvet. . ."*

In the front of the car she was supposed to be sitting up and looking straight out the window so she wouldn't get carsick and throw up. Carsick homesick gearshift heartsick. She had already thrown up before in the back seat on the way to Saskatchewan to visit her grandmother.

– I feel sick she said.

Her father had just lit a cigarette and puffed on it until it was burning bright red at the end and handed it to her mother. She put the unlit tip of her own cigarette against the bright burn of the lit cigarette handed him back his cigarette took a puff of her own and blowing smoke into the back seat said

– It's all in your imagination. Sit up. Look out the window.
– Can we stop?

She saw her father's eyes as he looked at her in the rearview mirror. He seemed mad.

– You're sure you feel sick? Are you making it up?
– Take some deep breaths her mother said.

She opened the back window and turned her head toward the fresh air. Breathing in and out and feeling the car moving and the noise of the radio and the cigarette smoke smelling sour and sharp and the sound of the engine.

– I still feel sick. Can we stop?
– I'm not stopping the car every two minutes her father said.
– She just wants some attention her mother muttered puffed her cigarette and blew the smoke to the roof of the Galaxie.
– Can we stop?
– Look out the window.
– Can we stop?
– We'll stop when we get to Lloydminster.

She felt hot and her ears were ringing and she could smell the cigarette smoke and then it was like her whole body turned cold and she threw up all over the floor the back of the seats the part of the back seat she was sitting on and all over her new pink skirt.

– Shit! Her father said looked in the rearview mirror flicked his cigarette out the window checking over his shoulder and flicked the signal light on.

Now they were stopped on the shoulder and she was bent over staring at her white shoes in case she was going to throw up any more. There was a spot on the toe of her shoe. She scraped it off on the gravel at the side of the road. Cars were going by like fire and spaceships a swooshing sound that moved the hot air to the side of the road and made her skirt flap.

– I feel way better now the girl said.

And her mother had wiped off the throw up with a blanket from the trunk and wet a corner with water she had in a thermos. Once the backseat was wiped off her mother put a towel over the spot and the girl sat back down. Her father waited for a break in traffic signaled looked over his shoulder and turned back onto the highway. The car was really stinky on the way to her grandmother's this time. They kept the windows open the whole way there.

When they passed a guy standing on the shoulder of the road holding up a piece of cardboard and the girl asked what it was and her father said it was S'TOON — short for Saskatoon. The girl's father stepped on the gas and when he passed the guy he yelled out the window.

– SUCKER! Hey maybe we should've stopped to pick him up. He could have sat in the puke on the backseat.

Her parents laughed and lit fresh new cigarettes and everything seemed okay again except for the smell in the car.

She pressed the buttons on the radio from station to station and at some stops there was no music at all just scratch and then she pressed all the buttons she could all at once and then back to pressing each one in turn. It was like typing on a typewriter. Keys of typewriter or buttons on a radio or keys of a piano.

Her father was holding the steering wheel with one hand and resting his arm on the door with the window open and a cigarette between his fingers and the wind. The sun was shining on his arm and the short plaid sleeve of his shirt was flapping in the wind as they drove on. The radio was playing and with her feet on the dashboard she could feel the drums and the guitars travel from the bottoms of her feet and all the way up her legs. It was like she was inside the radio in the car and the songs were inside her body.

– Put your legs down I don't want you to hit the gearshift her father said.

She wasn't quite sure what would happen but she imagined: the car might stop all of a sudden and they would go through the windshield and into the ditch or they would go backwards and her father wouldn't be able to steer properly and he would have to look back over his shoulder and they would end up in the ditch or the car would suddenly go so fast that the steering wheel would come off in her father's hands and he would start to shout and her mother would scream. She took her feet off the dash and tucked them under her. She sat up straight and looked out the front window. Another radio song buzzing in the blue dashboard. Christine hated it when the line on the radio dial wasn't quite on the station. It was fuzzy and faraway. She turned the button on the side to get the line and the number to match.

— We're losing that station her father said.

This was the part of the trip to her grandmother's when they switched from Alberta to Saskatchewan. It seemed everything got different all of a sudden. The road looked different. It got narrower and bumpier and the weeds and flowers got closer to the road. The sky had turned grey and soft and now tiny drops of rain were falling on the windshield already sprayed with dead bugs.

She sat back again as her father pressed in the cigarette lighter and then fiddled with the radio. Bits of songs and voices and static but finally he found a good station. *"Puff the magic dragon. . ."* and her father steered with one hand and looked from the road to the radio. There must be someone that can see us here in the car with the cigarettes and smoke and know that song is talking about us the girl thought. The cigarette lighter popped out of its hole like a little gopher. Her father grabbed it and the end was a red circle.

He steered and held the lighter to the tip of his cigarette puffing puffing and drawing in the smoke until the cigarette burned red too and then he snapped the lighter back in its place.

Christine put her feet back flat against the dashboard. She liked the rain and the grey sky. Her white socks against the blue dash and she could feel the buzzing of the radio and the thunder in the song travel from her feet up along her legs. *"Listen to the rhythm of the falling rain. . ."* This must be a song about us too she thought.

It rained the last time they had come to visit her grandmother on the farm. Her grandmother had phoned her mother long distance and said it had rained for three days straight. Now here they were parked on the gravel road that passed by her grandmother's farm. The long drive from the gravel road to her grandmother's house was just ruts and mud.

– We can't drive up or we'll get stuck her father said.

The girl could see the house at the top of the hill but from the gravel road to there it was just a muddy road and the big slough on either side of the road flooding the dip in the middle.

– Honk the horn and flash the lights someone will see us. We can just park on the shoulder here and walk in.

They waited in the car because the road was just way
too muddy to drive on and the windows were rolled
down and the smell of rain was coming in and her
mother and father lit cigarettes and it was already
getting dark or seemed to be dark already because
the light was so grey so grey and with the sky covered
by clouds so low they seemed almost on top of them.
- You wanted to come her father said and shoved the
  gearshift to the end of its narrow track.
- We'll just carry our suitcases to the house if we
  have to.
- Jesus Christ her father said and shook his head.
- Next time I'll just goddamn well come by myself.

Her father started honking the horn and puffing his
cigarette.
- Quit it!
- What? Someone will hear us, eh?

He started honking the horn again longer now and
leaning into the steering wheel and the girl thought
how the steering wheel was shaped like the big funnel
her mother used sometimes and she thought her father
might be so mad right now he would shrink himself
down and slide right into the middle of the steering
wheel and disappear. But he didn't disappear he just
kept honking the horn and smoking.

Was her father trying to play a tune on the steering wheel and using the horn as some kind of instrument? She listened hard as she had done so many times with other sounds she heard. She closed her eyes. Traffic on 66th street near their house the big trucks going by and the cars that would hum and rumble and she would listen for songs hidden in those sounds. Each tune was different even though the same things would make it every time. She would like to learn all the songs that cars and trucks and motorcycles made everywhere in the world and one day she would hitchhike across the country even though her mother said don't do it. She opened her eyes.

– Girls go thumbing and get picked up and they're never heard of again. Disappeared. Gone.

The girl hadn't heard that story before.

– Lots of girls who hitchhiked were picked up and they were kidnapped and stabbed or shot before they were dumped on a highway and left for dead. And they were the lucky ones! At least they lived to tell the tale her mother said.

Finally in the distance at the top of the hill coming out of the trees and turning onto the muddy road was the tractor with its big tires and noise and black smoke. Her uncle was driving it and she could see him bouncing up and down as the mud shot out from behind the tractor.

– Can we get out can we get out?
– No! Just stay in the car.
– You guys always bring the rain with you he said
to the girl's mother and hugged her with one arm.

Her uncle wore big green rubber boots and a big
yellow raincoat with the hood up over his head.
He held a big chain with a hook on each end in the
other hand.

The girl's father got out of the car. His hair was nicely
combed and he wore his nice shirt and brown cardigan
and his brown dress-up pants. Standing beside the car
now he pulled down the cardigan lit a cigarette and
threw the match on the road.
– Back up and I'll hook this to the bumper. We'll take
a run at it.

The girl was happy and excited to see her grandmother
and excited that they were going to be towed to the
house.

The tractor took off with black smoke puffing from it
and her uncle bouncing on the seat and all of a sudden
the car jerked forward.
– Have you got it in neutral? Her mother asked and
looked down at the gearshift.
– What do you think?

The tractor shot mud onto the windshield as it dragged the car behind her father gripping the steering wheel as the car moved from one edge of the muddy road to the other.

– Jesus Christ — this'll probably take the front end right off.

Her father spat out the window.

They were coming up to the dip in the road where the slough overflowed the road. Her uncle was going really fast now and the car seemed to float over this part of the road like a big blue boat. The windshield was covered in mud as they slowly climbed the hill to the house. Her father wasn't really driving the car was turned off just in neutral and the radio wasn't on. Her parents said nothing. Just stared straight ahead but at what? The windshield was covered with mud.

She had heard her parents talk about the car being good "clatteral" but she had never heard any kind of clatter from the car. It was a nice car she thought, anyway. Would it still be good "clatteral" covered with mud? Maybe she was missing something. Maybe there was something going on that she didn't know about. Maybe something was wrong she couldn't see. Only her parents could see it. If the bank called it "clatteral" maybe it was true. "Clatteral" was the word that went

through her mind. It made her think of the car keys
and their gold colour and the sound they made when
her father took them out of his pocket and turned
the key in the ignition. "Clatteral." Such a great word.
It tasted the sweet blue colour of the car and the key
and the car were more things that made her think
she could taste what she saw or taste what she felt the
world was or could be and it could all be described
on her tongue.

Christine looked behind over the back seat and through
the back window of the car and the road was a muddy
mess of ruts with water and fields on each side. Sunlight
began to break the clouds and when she turned back to
the front of the car and saw her parents looking at the
mud-covered windshield while her father tried to keep
the car on the road she thought she didn't know them
and they didn't know each other and the girl felt alone
even though they were in the same car and all going to
her grandmother's house.

Her uncle unhooked the chain from the tractor and
the front of the car.
- Better bring some more rain with you — the car
  could use a good wash her uncle said.
- I guess you made it her grandmother ran down the
  faded front steps and hugged everyone.

The dogs barked and her father brought their suitcases inside her grandmother's house, trying not to get his good shoes too muddy. The house always smelled the same: of wood and some kind of cleaner her mother never used and dust and dog and the steam of boiling water on the stove. The girl just let herself fall into the house into the pink light inside the house that matched this moment of her grandmother's happiness and her mother's happiness at being home.

Christine's grandmother had a cigarette in her hand.
– Well I guess you brought the rain with you! I've got the water on to boil she said. Tea or some coffee?
– Take your shoes off. Gramma doesn't need any extra work the girl's mother said.

They all put their muddy shoes on the sheets of newspaper spread out in front of the door.

Why did her uncle and her grandmother say they brought the rain with them? They didn't even try to do that. The kettle whistled and Christine's grandmother took it off the stove. She turned the knob and all the little blue fire fingers under the kettle disappeared. Christine saw curling smoke from a cigarette already burning by the sink.
– Gramma why are you smoking two cigarettes?
Her grandmother gasped like someone had said "Boo."

Girlie, I forgot about that one so it's a good thing you saw it. I wish I had your sharp eyes and sharp brain and she hugged the girl and kissed her on the cheek like she might never see her again and then she stubbed the yellow part of the cigarette which was the only thing left really besides a long trail of sad grey ash.

Her grandmother's kitchen was mostly the same as she remembered it. There was the silver pump beside the sink and the metal cup beside it. She opened the cupboard doors underneath and there was a big metal bucket that caught the dirty dishwater after her grandmother had done the dishes and pulled the brown rubber stopper from the drain.

– Stop snooping around her mother said.
– I want to make sure there aren't any mice the girl said but she was lying.

The last time she had opened those cupboard doors there had been a broken brown bowl a broken teacup with pink flowers on it but no matching plate and tins and bottles of all shapes and sizes. She wondered why her grandmother kept broken things. Why didn't she throw them away? The girl opened the knives-and-forks drawer and saw that there were spoons and knives and forks all mixed up together and only a few that had those little flowers on the handles. Most of the knives and forks looked different. Why didn't she have anything that matched?

- Out of there Christine! Her mother said. She closed the drawer and went back to the living room feeling caught out and that everyone was looking at her.

Her grandmother poured the water into a brown teapot that wasn't shiny anymore and put the lid on. Christine noticed the lid had a crack in it and had been glued back together.

Her grandmother poured water into two cups.
She took the cups into the livingroom and she and the girl's mother sat on the chesterfield with the T v on and talked about people with names the girl didn't know and they smoked cigarettes and had instant coffee in her grandmother's two nice tea cups that had no cracks or chips and that she kept up high in the back of the cupboard for special occasions. They had little pink flowers on them and gold trim and the girl thought these were very beautiful.
- Where's Daddy? The girl's mother said and she thought it was so funny to hear her grown-up mother call someone "Daddy."
- Haven't seen him since yesterday. He just takes off. Last time he brought some new-found friend of his home from the bar, they were both drunk as skunks, and I made up a bed for the guy on the couch. Be damned if he didn't piss himself.

Christine's mother laughed so hard she almost started crying and the girl was a bit afraid of what might happen. She'd never seen her mother laugh that much.

- I washed the cushion best I could let it dry and turned it over. You'd never know.
- I don't know how you put up with it Mom. I couldn't.
- You make your bed and you have to lie in it her grandmother said.

Christine decided she would never sleep on that couch again. Not after a stranger had peed on it. She thought that a grown-up peeing himself was sad. Sad for him and sad for her grandmother who cleaned up after he'd had his "accident." She didn't think it was funny that her grandmother had to do that. Why didn't her grandfather clean up his own friend's messes? That was the fair thing to do for her grandmother.

Christine's father and uncle sat at the kitchen table and they were laughing now too. The girl heard the uncle say he had a "26" and that he and the girl's father were going to throw the cork away tonight. She thought 26 had something to do with guns but it turned out it was whiskey.

Her father's voice and her uncle's voice were getting louder and they were laughing more and more and the air in the kitchen was getting so smoky and the ashtray that was a rusty cup on top and a brown plaid bean bag on the bottom was overflowing with stubbed cigarettes. Everyone else seemed to be laughing and having fun but her and she didn't know why. She wanted to say something funny but didn't know what.

- When's supper I'm getting hungry? she piped up. Her father's face changed he yelled at her from the kitchen and his voice got mean.
- Watch that mouth of yours! Use it to say sorry right now and stop putting on airs he said.
- Sorry Gramma and the girl sat right back in the chair bunching up the crocheted purple blanket that covered it. She looked at the television hoping she could just be invisible and they would forget about her and her mouth.

Christine's mother and grandmother kept talking in the living room about people whose names she didn't recognize. The news came on the T V and there were different people telling the stories at her grandmother's house different than the people who told stories on the news at home. The girl's father and uncle were talking and laughing again even louder than before and they were starting to swear. Her grandmother suddenly looked serious.

– Let's get some supper going it's later than I thought
 her grandmother said.

And her grandmother put margarine in the frying pan
and sliced bologna and fried it until it was crusty on
both sides and fried some potatoes from the fridge.
Then she cracked eggs in the pan and cooked them until
they were "hard as the sole of a work boot" which was
how her father said Christine's mother cooked, telling
her she would "boil it or fry it until I might as well chew
my work boot." The girl thought this was funny but it
had made her mother cry once when her father said it.
So the girl watched her mouth and didn't laugh now even
though she thought it might be a grown-up way to join in
with everyone and maybe they would forget her mouth.

– Now eat something and her grandmother filled
 plates and put them down in front of the girl's
 father and uncle. She set down plates for Christine
 and her mother.
– You certainly don't have to wait on me, Mom and she
 looked at the girl's father and uncle in a mean way.
– Sit by me Gramma the girl said.
– No honey, that's okay I'll just stand here. I need to get
 up and down anyway and her grandmother stood at
 the counter and smoked her cigarette and ate supper.
 But she didn't get up and down at all. She just stood
 at the counter and seemed nervous, watching the
 girl's father and uncle eat at the table and looking
 out the kitchen window every now and then.

Christine was sitting beside her mother who was not
talking or laughing at all just eating her supper fast
and looking down at her plate but her father's laughing
and swearing was getting so loud the girl was starting
to feel kind of scared. He never laughed like this at
home and he didn't swear this much.

–   We've barely made a dent in this bottle and we're
    finishing it off tonight and the girl's uncle filled up
    her father's cup with some more "26."
–   I told you I'm not drinking any more. . .but I'm not
    drinking any less either the girl's father said and
    laughed.
–   Okay I think you two have had enough. Put the cap
    on for tonight that's enough her grandmother said and
    she reached toward the table to get the bottle of 26.
–   Hey, we haven't had enough. We're nowheres near
    the bottom of the bottle her uncle said.
–   I don't want to spoil the party her father said and lit
    another cigarette.
–   It doesn't have to be a party. It's just us here.

The girl liked parties, especially birthday parties,
but she wasn't liking this party. She sat and tried to
be quiet and watch T v. It seemed this party was
mostly her grandmother telling her mother sad stories.
This visiting was boring. When they were being towed
up the driveway she thought something fun might
happen when they got to her grandmother's house.
So far things weren't that fun.

It was starting to get dark outside and the cool air was coming through the kitchen window. There was noise and laughing outside the house. They were men's voices.

– Well he knows to show up when the food's on anyways her grandmother said.

There was thumping on the front steps and then the door opened and Christine's grandfather came in with another man and their shoes were covered with mud. The girl didn't know the stranger but when her mother saw him come through the door her face changed. She seemed to know him from before but the girl wasn't sure if her mother looked angry or sad.

– Why the hell didn't someone come to tow us up? We were sitting in the car. . .

– You can go back and sit there some more her grandmother said to him.

– Come and give me a kiss.

– When hell freezes over.

– No lovin' at home and her grandfather turned to the other man who didn't laugh. The other man just looked at Christine's mother and she looked back at him. Christine thought her mother might cry.

– Hello Joan. How are you?

– Good — you Floydie?

– Good, good. Real good. He took his shoes off and set them outside on the porch. The girl noticed his

big toe was sticking out of a hole in his grey sock.
Her grandfather didn't bother to take off his shoes
all covered in mud.
- You're filthy take your shoes off! The girl's grandmother said.

But he came right into the kitchen with his muddy
footprints following him.
- Jesus Christ take your shoes off! Who the hell d'you
  think washes these floors?

Her grandfather ignored her grandmother and sat
down at the table.
- Well look who brought the rain with them. . . ?
  Her grandfather said to all of them and none of them
  but it was her mother that answered.
- Where've you been? the girl's mother said.
- Here, there, everywhere. Any supper?
- I'm sure Mom could've burnt it for you if she'd
  known when you were coming back.

Christine's mother crossed her legs rested her elbow
on the table and stared at him.
- Nothing she hasn't done before he said to the girl's
  mother.

Her grandmother was mad.
- I'm not cooking anything for you when you come
  home like this and such a filthy mess to boot.

I'll have to clean up after you I'm not going to drop everything so I can cook for you any damn time you feel like showing your face around here. . . nothing against you Floydie her grandmother said to the strange man.

– I think I should hit the road.
– Hit the road? It's mud! Don't let her scare you away.

Christine wasn't sure if her grandfather meant the man would be scared by her grandmother or her mother.

– Well look who's here! I didn't even see you there Beverly.
– No Dad, it's Christine the girl's mother told him.
– Oh, oh! Right! So many god-damn grand-kids. . . can't keep 'em straight! The girl's grandfather laughed. But no one else did.

He always got the girl's name wrong calling her by one cousin's name or another cousin's name or sometimes a name she didn't even know belonged to anybody. The girl missed her grandmother when she was at home in her own house but she never missed her grandfather when she was at home in her own house. He always seemed like a stranger to her and she had trouble imagining that he was her own mother's "Daddy."

– Floydie, have a drink for the road we'll play one hand of poker. C'mon, one hand.

She saw that the stranger and her mother were trying not to look at each other. Her mother just stared down at the cigarette package and turned it over and over. The stranger just stared at the trail of mud her grandfather had tracked in. They both looked sad. The stranger sat down at the kitchen table between her uncle and the grandfather.

– Is that your little girl?
– Yes. Christine? Come and say hello.

She didn't want to move from her spot. There was something about her mother when she was around this Floydie. She was happy to be watching Dick Tracy because it wasn't on back in Edmonton in Santa Rosa it wasn't on T V there. She pretended she didn't hear her mother but her mother was looking at her and she couldn't tell if she was kind of sad or scared or mad or everything at the same time so she went into the kitchen to meet the stranger to make her mother happy.

– What's your name?
– Floyd.
– My Mom called you Floydie.

He laughed.
– Yes. She's the only one who's ever called me Floydie. It started out as a joke. Your Mom was quite the joker when she was younger.

And everyone got quiet all of a sudden and the girl wondered why her mother only called him that name.

– Were you her boyfriend?

– Christine don't be rude!

– No, I wasn't your Mom's boyfriend. My brother was. . . a long time ago.

– What was his name?

– Frank.

– Does he still live at your house?

– No he passed away.

– Floydie. . .

– What did he die from?

– Something was wrong with his brain.

Her father wasn't even looking at the stranger just smoking his cigarette and listening to her uncle talk.

– Oh. Was all she could think of.

She went back to the living room to sit on the covered chair and she watched T V and tried to be quiet enough to hear what the grown-ups were saying.

– So I hear you haven't been home since yesterday. Don't you think you're getting too old for this Daddy? Christine's mother said.

– Oh you want me to be more like your mother?

– I'm not arguing with you.

– I drink to be sociable. See what you want to see. You're just too good for us out here now I guess. Like you've always been a little angel.

– I'm not arguing with you.

The grandfather and the other man started drinking "26" too and her grandfather said

– Bring out the cards and we'll take some money off my son-in-law. He's got more than I do!

Her father looked mad and flicked his cigarette into the ashtray.

– Aww I'm just yankin' yer chain! C'mon we'll play nickels and dimes.

And the girl heard the clank of silver on the table and the names of some of the games 'hooks and crooks' and 'one-eyed-jacks' or 'deuce is wild.' It was like they were talking another language and her father said

– Goddam nickels and dimes? What the hell? We'll play for a buck, maybe two bucks?
– Don't be stupid! Her mother said to her father.
– What? It's only a little poker! And he laughed.
– Someone's gonna lose money and there's always hard feelings.
– Don't lose our money Dad! the girl said.
– Don't be silly. I'm not going to lose anything.
– Well someone's going to lose some money. . .to hell with it.
– Deal a hand there her father said.

Something had changed and her mother was mad and not talking and her father was trying too hard to be funny and smile and he kept having more 26 and took some blue paper money out of his wallet.

The girl's mother called to her.

 — C'mon it's time for bed.

 — Where am I sleeping?

 — Upstairs.

 — By myself?

 — I'll be up right away.

The mother got the girl's pyjamas from the suitcase
and the two of them went into the bathroom which
was a room beside the kitchen and it had a sink with
a bucket under it and another bucket with a seat on top
of it to go to the bathroom in. When the girl's face was
all clean her mother told her to go pee and she lifted
the girl up on the bucket.

 — It stinks she said.

 — Don't put on airs. No one likes a person who puts
   on airs her mother said.

She said good-night to everyone but didn't give her
father a hug because she felt he wasn't being like her Dad
right now. She wasn't angry just a bit sad for him and for
her mother. Maybe for herself too. Her mother followed
her up the narrow stairs and tucked her into bed.

 — G'night. Go straight to sleep now.

And she tried but she could hear the voices downstairs
and the clank of silver in the pile on the table and
the rattle of glasses. She heard her grandmother say
"I'm going to bed don't burn the place down" and her

mother say "I'm going to bed too. Good-bye Floydie."
and then a noise on the stairs.

- Mom? Is that you?
- Get to sleep.
- I can't get to sleep.
- Well get to sleep now!
- Mom?
- What?
- Were you that man's girlfriend?
- No, his brother's girlfriend.
- How old were you?
- I was 16 and he was 19. Then he found out he was
  very sick.
- What was wrong?
- Cancer. A brain tumour. He was a nice boy.
- Was he?
- Yes, he was real nice.
- I wish he wouldn't have died Mom.
- Me too.
- Did you cry?
- I cried a lot.
- Did you know Dad then?
- I started going out with your Dad right after
  Frank died.
- Did Dad have a girlfriend?
- Dad had quite a few girlfriends.
- Was Dad Frank's friend?
- No they weren't friends at all. Your Dad didn't like
  him. He was jealous even then.

- I wish that Frank hadn't died.
- Me too. Now go to sleep.
- Were you going to marry him?
- I don't know. He never asked.
- But what if he did?
- Go to sleep.
- Are you going to bed right away Mom?
- Pretty soon. I'll go say good-bye to Floydie. He looks so much like his brother.
- I'm still thinking about that boy with the brain tuber.
- "Tumour." Just go to sleep and try to forget about it. I'll leave the stair light on okay?
- Okay Mom.

Her mother kissed her.
- Goodnight see you in the morning.
- See you in the morning, in the morning, in the morning Mom.

She lay there trying not to think about the boy who died but she couldn't forget it. Her Mom had a boyfriend who died. Did she love him? Her father had a lot of girlfriends before he married her Mom. Did he love them? What would have happened if they had married different people? Would she be the same person? Who would she be living with? Her father and one of his girlfriends? Her mother and Floydie's brother Frank? It made her sad to think about. Who would she be now? Would she look the same and think the same? There were some things, important things that happened before her. Before she was born her parents had been young teenagers and before that little kids like her and before that babies and before that? She didn't understand it. Things that happened to her mother before her. Things that happened to her father. She didn't understand it but she would try her hardest to.

She listened to the voices and the laughing and the sound of the cards being shuffled and coins clinking like keys on the hard table downstairs and she knew she wasn't alone. But there in the dark under the blankets with the plastic curtain blowing away from the window screen and back to it again away and back she felt that there was only herself in this world and those voices that sounded like the cold water she drank from the tin cup at her grandmother's sink were something she couldn't hold on to and couldn't keep. The voices would get out and go to the same place as before she was here. The place where her parents came from before she was here. Maybe they would be happy there.

She woke up and it was Sunday morning and sunlight was grey and soft coming in the little window in the room. She could hear the radio downstairs but her mother was still asleep.

It was a choir singing songs and it was such a sound that she felt it when she breathed it was so beautiful and red of course there was red from the first few notes she heard this morning and they were in her world. Red had the taste of these songs and it was the way she felt in her world. What was it that she was supposed to forget? Oh yes, her Mom's boyfriend had died of cancer in the brain and her Mom had been sad. Christine ran down the narrow stairs and she tried not to feel sad. She liked her grandmother's house even if it had a stinky bathroom.

She sang under her breath.

— Happy in this house happy in a small house small houses happy happiest.

It was the middle of May but it seemed to the girl it should be Christmas. The house was warm enough so it was easy to know it wasn't winter and yet she still felt as if it should be Christmas. She wanted it to be Christmas. Why couldn't it be Christmas at this precise moment and she wished for the house to be filled with red and green and the taste of the colours would burn her lips and she could swallow those colours red and green.

This morning she crouched under the arborite table speckled with tiny silver stars. As she thought of them they exploded with the taste of metal in her mouth. Tasting like metal on her tongue.

But she thought of the winter when she tried to figure out the trick her father first showed her.
– Blackbird blackbird fly away home.

Where did the little piece of paper on his fingernails disappear to? He moved his fingers so fast so fast but there it was and then it was gone again. This piece of paper stuck to the nails on his fingers. She couldn't tell where the birds went. First they were sitting on her father's fingers in winter and it might have been Christmas. Her father made her laugh that time.
– Blackbird blackbird fly away home.

Happiness. Red. Love. Red. Anger. Red. Sadness. Red. Fear. Red. Never just the three-letter word she had first learned. She knew now that these three letters or maybe every letter or maybe even every word could never describe exactly.

This morning her grandmother was quiet and her father was quiet and everyone else was still asleep it seemed. Her grandmother and her father were quiet and not laughing or asking each other any questions.

But she was crouched under the arborite table with
the top that was speckled with tiny silver stars. As she
thought of those stars just above her she imagined they
exploded with a taste of metal in her mouth, metal on
her tongue.


Her father leaned bent over and looked at her under
the table.
—  How about that trick? he said.
—  Okay and the girl was so happy.

She crawled from under the stars on the table and stood
beside him. Her father had done this trick before. He tore
tiny pieces of paper and drew little birds on them with a
pen. The birds were just little sticks with wings but the
girl thought they were beautiful because her father had
drawn them and she knew what they were right away.
Then he put each piece of paper on his tongue and stuck
each bird to a finger on each hand. He tapped his fingers
on the table to the rhythm of the song.
—  Blackbird blackbird fly away home.
    Blackbird blackbird fly away home.

When the song was finished and his fingers came to
rest on the table of stars the birds were gone. Where did
the little birds on his fingers disappear to? He moved his
fingers so fast so fast the birds were there and then gone
just like before.

– Blackbird blackbird fly away home.
 Blackbird blackbird fly away home.

He sang and the birds were back again. His fingers were
moving so fast she couldn't see what changed couldn't
tell if there was a bird sitting on his fingers just like at
Christmas. A fingernail or a bird. She still couldn't tell.
Her father made her laugh this time too.
– Blackbird blackbird fly away home.


Her father said he had to get back to his job in Edmonton.
And after breakfast they were like birds flying on the way
back home to Edmonton already and even though she
was missing her grandmother and the chickens and the
chicken coop and the eggs and the water in the tin cup
she was happy to be sitting in the front seat of the car.
Her father had let her put the key in the ignition but he
said he would turn it. Still she liked the way the key fit
and how it seemed to scrape a bit before it locked itself
inside the steering wheel.


She did not want to be carsick this time. It seemed better
now there was no sick feeling in her stomach her ears
weren't buzzing and she wasn't sweating but maybe she
was getting bored.

On the way back her parents said nothing. The radio
was on and she sat in the front seat again so she wouldn't
get sick. Her mother read a book and sat as far away
from her father as she could.

- What book is that Mom?
- *The Harrad Experiment.*
- Can you read it to me?
- No, it's not for kids.

Her mother told her movie magazines weren't really
for kids but she told Christine about Elizabeth Taylor
who was Cleopatra and Richard Burton who was in
that movie too and her mother said he had left his
wife and Liz had left her husband who had already left
someone else for her. Christine never got tired of that
story. Her mother explained they got a divorce which is
where you can stop being married but only if you want.

- I don't know why they even bother getting married
  in Hollywood. Their kids must be so messed up.

And her mother shook her head.

Christine thought it might not be that bad to have
movie stars for parents. There were shots in the
magazines of movie stars and their kids walking
in airports or posing on skis with matching outfits
and big sunglasses. They were smiling. Christine
had never been on a plane and never been skiing.

That might be fun. And in the movie magazines women wore beautiful clothes and big sunglasses that almost covered their faces.

She hoped that her mother didn't still love the dead boy Frank, but hoped she still loved her father.

She thought of the little disks hidden in her closet and under her bed and at the back of her drawers. They were her secret. The disks were how she could make people and things that happened something real. The disks she made let her hold those times and remember them forever. Like the putty her father had used to fill the nick in the cupboard, her disks filled the empty space that was left behind when a moment was over. Her mother and father could never find them.

*The girl climbed up on the kitchen counter and took down the blue M E L M A C cup. She set it on the counter but this time she used a knife to mix the powder and water. She had been told not to touch those knives, the ones that man came to the house and sharpened at the kitchen table. But she took one when her mother and sister were still sleeping. Afraid to touch the sharp blade, she slowly stirred until the putty was stiff and then rolled a small ball between her palms. She flattened it to a disk and then eased the tip of the shiny silver blade. . .once. . .twice. . . into the top. The blade made two clean lines an* L.
*Of course she recognized this letter it was the beginning of* L M N O P *and it was the first letter in Lemon, Little Bo Peep, and Liz Taylor. When she pulled out the knife a bit of putty stuck to the tip and she thought of it again. During the day it wasn't bad. The sun was bright, she was busy and thinking about other things. But when it started to get dark and quiet, it would come back to her — the knives, the blood on his white robes. Every time she thought about it she felt her stomach turn over and her throat tighten. She couldn't stop thinking about it now. As she made this disk she thought how much she wanted to forget what she had seen. She hid it at the back of her closet and hoped one day she would stop remembering.*

Christine's mother bought magazines with movie stars on the covers. The magazines were made of smooth, shiny paper with pictures of beautiful women with shiny dresses and beautiful hair and smooth eyebrows and long eyelashes and red lipstick and sometimes sunglasses. They were with handsome men with suits and ties and perfect hair that waved up in front and faces that never had any whiskers. Christine and her sister liked to look at the movie stars and her favourite was Elizabeth Taylor who was one of the movie stars on those magazine covers and she was beautiful with purple eyes. Her mother said Elizabeth Taylor had been married a lot and now she was married to a guy named Eddie Fisher who she stole from Debbie Reynolds but then she met Richard Burton in a movie called *Cleopatra* but outside the movie Elizabeth Taylor was still married to Eddie but she fell in love with Richard Burton who was already married to somebody else too.

Christine's mother told her stories about the movie stars and the girl knew their names and remembered the movies they were in and what they wore and who they were married to so she felt she knew these people. Her sister was too little to remember or really care, but Christine thought maybe they might even come to their house in Santa Rosa to visit one day. Christine would curl her hair and wear her best dress. Her mother said that would never happen because Hollywood was a long way from Edmonton and the Santa Rosa neighbourhood. But Christine imagined that she would meet a movie star one day or she might even be a movie star herself one day or she might even marry a movie star.

Every afternoon after lunch when the house was quiet and her sister was sleeping Christine and her mother would watch black and white movies. They were old but didn't scare her they made her sad in some ways and happy in other ways. When she watched the black and white movies with her mother it was quiet in the small pink house and her mother wasn't busy or worried or smoking she just lay on the chesterfield with a blanket and her cigarette package on the coffee table beside the ash tray. Her sister was sleeping but Christine was awake and her mother was awake and they were quiet and together and the little pink house was cool and her mother didn't answer the phone if it rang and Christine felt that she and her mother and the movie stars in the black and white movie they were watching on TV were all connected in this moment. When the movie started and the words came on the TV screen and the names of the movie stars

were there. Her mother read them out to her Spencer
Tracy, Joan Bennett, Elizabeth Taylor and the movie
was *Father of the Bride.* The movie was funny and happy
and the people all loved each other even though they
argued and even the arguments were funny in a way.
And when Elizabeth Taylor wore her wedding dress
and her veil she was all in white and shiny and lacy and
she looked like a queen. Christine looked at her mother
and father's wedding picture on top of the blue T V and
thought how nice they looked and she and her mother
stayed on the chesterfield the whole time and were
quiet. When the movie was over her mother sat up
and lit a cigarette.

– Elizabeth Taylor is so pretty Christine said.
– Maybe we'll go see *Cleopatra.* I'd like to see it.
– Downtown?
– No, we'll go to the drive-in.


They would go and Christine was happy. Now Christine
had seen Liz Taylor in *Father of the Bride* but she had
already seen her dressed up as Cleopatra on the cover
of one of her mother's movie magazines. Her mother
had said it was playing at the Star-vue Drive-in and they
could go this Friday after her father came home from
work and got cleaned up. When the *Cleopatra* ad came
on T V Christine couldn't believe it. Cleopatra wore
a gold crown and a gold dress and the little boy beside
her was all in gold and there were dancers and smoke

and the people in the crowd wore robes and Cleopatra
was beautiful so everyone looked at her and Christine
thought she could live in that world if she had to pick
a place to go to in her mind.


After supper, every night that week Christine looked in
the newspaper for the muddy black and white ad for the
Star-vue Drive-in ad: *CLEOPATRA*. Elizabeth Taylor.
Richard Burton. Rex Harrison. So when Friday came
she started looking out the kitchen window for her father
to come home from work as soon as her mother started
to make supper.
 - When will he get here? Will the drive-in start
   without us?
 - He'll be here when he gets here. Don't worry the
   movie won't start until dusk.
 - What's dusk?
 - Not quite day and not quite night.

Christine felt as if she were in between waiting on
something on one side of going to the drive-in and the
other. When she saw her father turn into the driveway
she ran to the back screen door and jumped up and
down waving at him. He seemed to take forever to stub
a cigarette in the ashtray get his lunch kit and plaid jacket
out of the back seat and replace his hat on his head.
 - Dad! Dad! We've got to hurry if we want to get to
   the drive-in on time!

- I've gotta wash-up and we need to have supper. . .
- We'll go before it turns dusk, right Dad?
- Yep, pretty soon.
- I get to stay up late for the drive-in, right Dad?

Her mother answered
- You can get into your pyjamas before we go and you and your sister can sleep in the back seat if you get tired. We'll bring pillows and blankets for you.

Christine would not close her eyes until the movie was over. She was so excited to see *Cleopatra* at the drive-in.

Everyone was moving so slowly it seemed. The table was set and they ate their macaroni and pork chops but no dessert because they would have treats at the drive-in and then her father went to wash-up and her mother cleaned the table and did the dishes and Christine went and got changed into her pyjamas so no one would have to ask her and she came and sat at the kitchen table so her mother would see she was ready to go.
- Lift your feet she told Christine as she swept under the table.
- Can we go now?
- I'm not coming home to a dirty house her mother said.

She could hear her father whistling and the hangers
in the closet clanking together and one falling on the
floor. "Shit," he muttered. Finally her father came into
the kitchen in his good pants and shiny shoes and his
nice plaid shirt with his hair combed and he had shaved
and had a little piece of white toilet paper on his chin
that was soaked through with bright red blood.

- Can we go now?
- Yes bring your pillow.
- What shoes should I wear?
- Your flip-flops will be fine.
- Head out crew her father always said this when he
  was happy and Christine thought he seemed just
  like her and just as happy just as glad to be going
  to the drive-in.

Her father locked the back door with a cigarette in
his mouth and Christine walked in front of him and
behind her mother who carried her little sister and she
thought of the *Cleopatra* ad on T V and imagined she
was Cleopatra wearing all gold and her flip-flops were
gold sandals and in the backseat she could see some
pink in that blue sky and she thought this must be
the beginning of dusk. They would make it on time
for *Cleopatra*. "*Can't get used to losing you. . .*" was on
the radio and she loved that Andy Williams voice and
the ticking and plucking sounds in that song.

They were outside the city now and driving down a gravel road with tall trees on either side and they were driving behind other cars and there were cars and dust following them too. When Christine saw the big white screen in the distance she was so happy she told her parents she loved them and they laughed and said they loved her too and she thought they loved each other as well and when they got to the gate there was a big sign that said Sky-vue Drive-in in blue lights and it had a shooting blue star that blinked on and off. There was a little building with a man sitting behind a window and her father said "Family" to him and gave the man two blue bills. They pulled away and Christine saw rows of silver poles with silver tops.

– Not too far from the concession her father said.

– I want to be able to see the screen her mother said.

They decided on a spot close to the concession and right in the middle of the row. Her father rolled down the window and took the silver top from the pole and hooked it on to his window. He rolled it all the way up.

– This okay? he asked

– Fine her mother said.

– When will it start? Christine said.

– People are still coming in it won't be for a few minutes it's still pretty light.

– I'm going to the concession want anything? her father said.

– I'm coming too!

— Get me a coffee and some popcorn her mother said.

Christine followed her father with her flip-flops slapping her feet and crunching the fine gravel underfoot.

The concession was bright with signs that had pictures of corn on the cob, pickles, hamburgers, hot dogs and a big red Pepsi-Cola sign in swirly white letters. They bought popcorn and Pepsi and her father got a coffee for her mother and a corn on the cob and a cream soda and an Oh Henry chocolate bar and a Cuban Lunch chocolate bar and a popcorn and Pepsi for Christine. They carried their concession cargo back to the car just as the drive-in began. It was little boxes of popcorn with feet and glasses of pop with feet singing and telling people to go to the concession and then there was an ad that told people not forget to replace their speakers on the metal pole when they left. Christine looked at the car beside them. There were two teenagers in it and they were taping newspaper over the windows.
— What are those people doing Dad?
— They just want it to be really dark when they watch the movie.

Christine saw her father look over at her mother and smile. But Christine didn't think it was so funny. It wouldn't make any difference if it were dark in their car, it needed to be dark outside to see the movie better.

The screen went black and then there was loud music and yellow and red letters swirled onto the screen.

– Is Cleopatra starting Mom?

– That says, Feature Presentation.

Finally, *Cleopatra* was starting. There were men in armour and men in robes and a lot of talking in a way that Christine thought was old-fashioned and boring but then Elizabeth Taylor rolled out of a big rug and she was Cleopatra. Was that what Cleopatra really looked like? And she and Caesar fell in love and she had a son and Caesar had to go back to Rome.

Then Cleopatra came to visit him in Rome and the baby was a little boy now and there were dancers and music and people cheering and there were puffs of red smoke and puffs of yellow smoke and she and the little boy were riding on a big animal and then they were carried down so Caesar could see them. Christine was getting bored. A lot of talking and walking around. There were no funny parts at all.

Then Cleopatra was looking into a fire and there was a witch and Caesar was on the steps in his robes and the other guys were in their robes and they

stabbed him again and again and there was blood
and he held out his hand to his friend Brutus to help
him but Brutus stabbed him too. Why wasn't he his
friend? Caesar saved his life and Caesar was his friend
and Cleopatra knew something was wrong and she
fainted from what the fortuneteller witch told her.
Christine covered her eyes and her heart was beating
and she wished she had never seen that part. If only
she had looked the other way, if she had been in the
concession or in the bathroom. Her sister had fallen
asleep and didn't see it. She was lucky not to have seen
the stabbing. Christine wished she'd been asleep so
she wouldn't have seen the blood and the knives and
the way that Caesar held out his hands to his friend
for help and he stabbed him. Why hadn't Cleopatra
stopped him from going to get stabbed if she knew
from what the witch said? Then the screen went black
and the sound stopped and her mother read the word
on the screen: INTERMISSION.

Christine asked if she could go to the bathroom.
And her father took her and she held his hand and
she walked with him in the dark in between the cars
and looked inside and there were people talking and
laughing and kissing and eating popcorn and drinking
their pop and they didn't seem to care that Caesar's
own friends had stabbed him.

Over and over and even when he put his hand out. . .

The concession was bright with yellow light and Christine squinted against it. She didn't even care about the posters for popcorn or corn on the cob or Pepsi-Cola. In the bathroom she waited in line and didn't even care. The doors were painted blue and she clicked the little silver bolt lock shut. She just stood there thinking about Julius Caesar. If this bathroom could be a time machine she would travel back and save him. If she was Cleopatra she would have kept him home that day and if she was one of his friends she would have helped him and taken his hand. She made sure she didn't sit on the toilet seat and she washed her hands and pulled down the cloth towel until she found a clean dry part and dried her hands. Her father was waiting outside the door smoking a cigarette and Christine didn't want him to think that anything was wrong so she asked if she could have another Pepsi and some licorice and her father said okay sure and he bought another Cuban Lunch and a coffee for her mother. They walked back to the car and Christine's legs felt shaky and her stomach felt sick. She couldn't stop thinking about the blood and the stabbing and Caesar's face. Her flip-flops slapped her feet and crunched on the gravel. When they got back to the car the movie had started again but Christine didn't even care anymore. She didn't care about Elizabeth Taylor all she could think about was the knives and the blood.

Someone threw a spear and killed Cleopatra's friend and he fell down and died and then the whole thing turned into a painting.

– When is the movie over? When are we going home?

– Go to sleep if you're tired her mother said.

She wasn't tired. She sat up and tried to watch the movie resting her chin on the seat. There was more talking and fighting and ships in the ocean and more fighting and Mark Anthony wanted to die and Christine didn't understand what was going on anymore. There was a lot of killing and more talking and there was a war. Even Cleopatra's little boy was killed and Mark Anthony stabbed himself and Cleopatra was so sad she killed herself too by letting a snake bite her. Christine felt relieved when the movie was finally over and the scene changed to a painting but she wished she'd never been so excited to go to the drive-in and she wished her parents hadn't taken her. She just wanted to leave the drive-in and go home.

Her father hung the speaker back on the pole and they slowly drove out the gates and when Christine looked ahead and behind her the trail of car lights reminded her of the lines of soldiers in *Cleopatra* and the people who had brought Cleopatra into the city and she thought of Caesar being stabbed again.

Christine thought about Caesar and all that blood as soon as she woke up and it made her feel sick again and scared.

When she came into the kitchen it was already late in the morning because she had slept in and her mother said
– What's wrong?
– Nothing.
– You look peaked. Are you feeling okay?
– No.
– What is it?
– I'm thinking about the movie. I thought I would forget by today but I can't Christine said.
– What about the movie?
– The stabbing and the blood when Caesar died.
– It's not real. They just use ketchup.
– Did it happen for real in history?
– Well, yes it did happen but in the movie it wasn't real.
– But why did people do that to Caesar for real? Those men were supposed to be his friends. If they didn't want him to be the king anymore they could have just said. They didn't have to stab him so many times. Wasn't Brutus supposed to be his friend?
– Yes, but Brutus betrayed him in the end.
– Why?
– Sometimes people want to be important I guess.

Christine's father came out of the bathroom rubbing the shaving cream from his face and said
– What's going on? In a joking way.
– She's upset about the movie last night. . .when Caesar was stabbed.

Christine thought there might be more than that, but she wasn't sure she even knew what it was or if she could even tell her parents.
– Uh-oh, tsk her father said trying to be happy.
  I have to go to the store for some smokes and I need a little sidekick to come with me, okay?

And Christine said she would even though she hadn't had breakfast yet but she didn't care. She wasn't even hungry.

Her father held her hand as they walked toward 66th street.
– Okay, the coast is clear her father said and they walked across to the Santa Rosa Grocery with its grey shingles and rusty chimney and stairs going up the outside to a little door on the top floor.

Christine got to the door before her father and there it was. A blue five dollar bill flapping like a blue salmon trapped in the cold silver metal door frame of the

corner store. When she saw the five dollar bill flapping
in the hard metal she tasted lemon just for a moment,
then picked up the bill and gave it to a woman who
had walked through the door just ahead of her.
A little gust of wind as she opened the door lifted
the bill and sucked it upward to meet the point of the
blue chiffon scarf at the back of her head holding down
her black hair stretched around brush rollers the size
of fingers.

– I think this is yours?

And the stout woman ahead of her in the shiny-
smooth royal blue and white baseball jacket with LIZ
marking her left shoulder turned to look at her. She
was not really a stranger because Christine could read
the name on her jacket. This Liz grabbed the bill from
the girl's hand with a sudden twist like she was taking
a fish off a hook or like she thought the money stunk
or something but smiling anyway in case Christine
might change her mind.

– Aren't you a little sweetheart? She said quietly and
  then shouted at the man at the counter
– Hi Jimmy! How're ya?
– Good, good! What can I do ya for?
– Just gotta pick up a coupla things.

She disappeared between shelves of toilet paper and
Comet and s o s pads and thread and canned meat
and Kraft Dinner.

– What did you do that for? The girl's father bent to
whisper right in her face. We could have used that
money! She saw his face seem to melt and become
part of hers when she looked up at the convex
mirror at the top corner above the last aisle.
– I-I-I thought it was hers.
– Did you see her drop it? Did you?
– I don't remember now. I think I did.
– If you didn't see her drop it then it's yours.
Sometimes I wonder.

Just then Christine looked toward the mirror and
it seemed to her it was just like a movie. She saw
a quick flash of bright silver and blue reflected as
this Liz quickly put a can of salmon in her pocket.
Christine saw her. She knew she saw her even
though Liz pretended she hadn't.

Christine's father had lit a cigarette now and was up
by the cash register trying to choose between a Cuban
Lunch or Turkish Delight chocolate bar flicking ash on
the floor and blowing out a big puff of smoke. He was
talking to Jimmie behind the counter as he pressed
the cash register buttons saying out loud the little blue
numbers on the tin of sardines and turning a loaf of
bread her father was buying like he was seeing it for
the first time, but he was busy talking to Christine's
father and saw nothing of Liz's distorted reflection in

the mirror. So Christine stood close to her father and said quietly to the man

- Excuse me mister but I just saw that woman there take something.
- 'scuse me?
- I saw that lady there take something from your shelf. A can of something.

He looked at Christine's father. He looked at Christine.

- You sure little girl?
- I saw her.
- You're absolutely sure?

Christine thought this was the right thing to do to make up to her father for not keeping the five dollar bill and the right thing to do for Jimmie by telling him his friend Liz was taking things from him.

- I saw her in the mirror.

And the man looked up at the mirror and the woman was just standing there turning over a box of SOS pads and looking serious. In that moment Christine hated this Liz for taking the five dollar bill and not giving it back to her. It wasn't Liz's money to take. She should have given it to Christine and she would have given it to her father and he wouldn't have been mad. Liz should have said No, sweetheart you keep it. You found it.

- I saw her in the mirror. She put the can in her pocket. I saw her. In the mirror.

Everything suddenly got very quiet and Christine's stomach felt like it did when Cleopatra opened that basket and there was a snake moving around in it under some pieces of fruit.

Liz brought a box of s o s pads and matches to the cash. Jimmy looked at her and smiled and Christine's father took Christine's hand and said
– C'mon time to go.

Christine was looking at Liz but she ignored her and smiled a big smile at Jimmy. She was wearing blue fuzzy slippers. Christine hated her. Why was she wearing curlers and slippers outside? She wasn't a kid she was a grown-up and they didn't wear their pyjamas or slippers out not even to a drive-in.
– Anything else you want me to ring through Liz? Jimmy said.
– What d'ya mean Jimmy? No, just this.
– You sure about that Liz? You're a good customer. You sure about that Liz?
– What d'you mean Jimmy?
– Can I please take a look inside your purse there Liz?
– What? and she laughed a nervous sort of laugh.
– Open up your purse Liz.

She looked at Christine and whispered "You little. . ." she didn't finish the sentence but Christine knew she wasn't going to say sweetheart this time.

Liz reached into her pocket and there it was. The can of salmon.

– Oh, Jeez. . .sure Jimmy. Must've just fallen in there.
– I've got that Liz.
– Gee, thanks Jimmy. Sure, go ahead and ring that in. Not sure how it got into my pocket.
– I saw you put it there Christine said looking at Jimmy and then at Liz.
– C'mon time to go and Christine's father laughed a nervous laugh.
– But I saw her Dad. I did.
– Your kid needs to learn some manners she said to Christine's father.
– You need to learn not to steal from your friends, lady her father said.
– I wasn't stealin' nothin'! It fell into my purse.
– No you put it in there Christine said
– You lippy little brat. . .

Christine closed her eyes hunched her shoulders held her breath bracing for the slap she thought was coming. She could feel her heart beating fast and her stomach was feeling the way it did when she was carsick. She couldn't move. Her legs felt numb and she just stood there not sure what was coming next.

– What do you think you're doing? Christine's father stepped in front of Christine blocking the space between her and the woman.
– Someone needs to take that girl down a peg. . .

- Seems to me she's just telling the truth.
- That mouth of hers is going to get her into trouble one of these days.
- Worry about your own troubles lady.
- I don't have to stand here and listen to this bullshit. The woman looked at Jimmy waiting for him to say something but he just asked if she wanted her receipt. The woman grabbed the box of S O S, the matches and the can of salmon and walked quickly out the store. Her slippers slapping the scuffed linoleum. The screen door slammed behind her.
- Sorry about that Jimmy.

Christine didn't know why her father would say sorry when it was the woman who should have said sorry for stealing and for being so mean.
- Y'know she takes as much as she pays for but I never say anything.
- Well you know kids and Jimmy and Christine's father both laughed though Christine didn't know what was funny. Her legs and arms still felt shaky.
- That's okay she did right by telling.

If she did right by telling why wasn't there a different ending to things? Why didn't Jimmy tell the woman off, chase her out of the store or call the police?
- Thanks there Jimmy her father said.

Jimmy rang in the Cuban Lunch and the sardines and the loaf of bread and put them in a small brown bag with the bread on top so it wouldn't get squished.

– Come again he said to them.

Christine's father carried the paper bag in one arm and he held the door open for Christine. The spring that kept the door from flapping open was stretched as far as it could go. As they waited to cross the street Christine asked her father:

– Why didn't that woman say sorry to Jimmy for stealing?
– Maybe she felt ashamed.
– Why didn't she say sorry to me then? I was telling the truth.
– Truth or not, sometimes it's better just to keep your mouth shut.

epilogue

Slowly.

Slowly now the moon was being painted over with
red. Awash in the colour. The girl could still see just
a bit of the moon on top, a simple shape that glowed
and shone and shone.

There were other things the girl thought of as she
watched red being slowly pulled across the surface
of the moon: her mother pulling the soft red blanket
over her when she pretended to be asleep, the colour
red closing over the shape of the moon like the lid
of an eye, the moon like a cross-section of an eye.

The girl saw a program on T v. The cornea. The iris.
The lens. Vitreous humour. Aqueous humour.
A different kind of humour though. Not the funny
kind of humour because there was nothing funny
about the eye, because there was nothing funny
about losing both eyes or even one eye. She was
afraid of what it would be like to lose her sight and
how horrible it would be to wake up one morning
and be blind.

She would draw her own diagram of an eye. The cornea could shine and she would colour the vitreous humour and aqueous humour red. Draw and label the parts of the eye. Sideview. Cross-section. Ha! Such humour!
– Knock knock. Who's there? Europe. Europe who? No you're a poo.

She would sharpen her red pencil crayon to the sharpest tip she could possibly get. Maybe she would only write with red pencil crayon. Sometimes she hated just using her plain old lead pencil, especially when she was drawing. She couldn't make things look real and she would feel so angry. When she drew a face the nose the eyes the ears never looked the way they did in her mind. When she tried to draw faces from the side they looked flat and she felt she should be able to see the other eye the other ear the other side of the face but it looked so stupid when she did that.

But when she was printing letters now, she loved her lead pencil. The way the pencil point would slide up and down the sticks and circles of B and D and C and J and scratch across the surface of the paper. She could hear the sound each letter made on her paper. The letters and the words whispered to her, not just what she was reading but something else. Some other meaning something beyond each letter and each word. There was a colour she could feel and taste and a story that she could hear that came out of each letter and every word she wrote.

She just knew it.
She had dreamt about it.

There were black letters on a big white parachute and
the story written on it covered the tree in her backyard,
in her dream she looked up at it and the wind was
blowing her hair in every direction at once and she
could feel its invisible cold reaching to touch her neck
and her shoulders but in the dream the tree stood
perfectly still.

The black letters made words that made sense no matter
how she read them: top to bottom left to right or right to
left or around and around the tree latitude and longitude
and she knew these words now and she knew this story.
But it wasn't a real parachute that covered the tree.
She knew this story covering the tree was on paper and
not silk. Branches and leaves poked from underneath the
white covering. In the dream she wondered if they were
trying to rip the paper canopy, or maybe the leaves and
branches were just trying to breathe.

This was pure. She was able to read each letter and each
word any way she wanted top to bottom, left to right,
bottom to the top, right to left. She could read round and
round and as she flew she could follow the words and
make something out of them. She was flying around the
tree and the wind carried her and she felt its weight in
her dream but she was weightless.

But when she tried to reach for the black letters on the white paper they began to disappear. She knew she had to hurry to gather everything on the paper, the words and letters and the story and she was flying and so the paper and the letters and the words were just out of her reach she kept closing her fingers but she grasped nothing. The words disappeared and the paper disappeared.

She must remember them she must remember must remember remember.

The stars were shining so bright. There for the counting. 1-2-3-4-5-6-7-8-9-10 but then she lost count. Now she had to think of something else. A marble. Yes, the moon was a marble shining in the snow like the games of marbles in the snow in winter.

A circle around the moon. A circle in the snow. Where everyone would shout and then try to knock the other marbles out of the circle. The eclipse was like the murky red-orange marble. The solid. The solid red-orange marble that everyone had wanted but she had gotten by luck in the bag her Mother had bought from Army and Navy. They rubbed the snow off the marbles so they would roll better. So they could pick up speed and strength.

Christine thought she could brush the snow off the top of the moon. There it shone. So bright. *"Star light star bright first star I see tonight wish I may wish I might have the wish I wish tonight. . ."* That must be snow on the moon. So bright. So bright reflecting the sun she had learned at school but the sun was so far away it could not melt the snow.

Watching and watching. The ring around the moon. The red covering the moon like a marble. She was tired and her neck hurt. The bright moon was almost covered with red. Then it was gone covered in a dusting of red.

The kitchen lights were turned off and there was only the light from the stars and the disappearing moon out of the dark. She could smell the kitchen the dust from their days the smell of bread and rhubarb jam and milk and when the furnace came on with a soft breath she felt its warmth. Yes that dust must be coming up from her house and reaching the moon and covering it with soft red.

She could feel the red pencil crayon in her hand. Red. Then she knew she could hear the sound of her pencil making the song of letters and words on the page and she wasn't sure which she liked better the colour red or letters and words. The sound of letters and words.

MOON. ECLIPSE. RED. R E D.
She loved to write those letters made of sticks and curves.
R E D. Red.

She remembered one Sunday evening: in front of the
T V dancing in her favourite red housecoat and she had
rags in her hair so she could have curls in the morning.
In her mind the eclipse and the dancing and the words
and the colour were all one thing now.

And in this moment she so loved that colour red
covering the moon and she so loved the way the
curtains in the kitchen were open wide so she could
see the sky and the moon and she could imagine red
and the letters and the words. But then the moon
disappeared and where its shape had been was the
feeling she had suddenly become heavy in this room
and her parents were strangers and she was a stranger
to them and she hated them for that and she thought
if she ever wanted to she could paint herself out of
this life and disappear or she could write herself into
this life or make herself reappear somewhere else.
Like the eclipse of the moon like the shape of the
disks she had made and hidden.

Christine went to her bedroom and opened the closet door. She got down on her hands and knees and moved the red vinyl padded box where her mother had kept the old vacuum. It was her toy box now. There in the dark corner at the back of her closet were disks she had made out of her father's wood putty. She picked them up and blew off the dust. She held them in her hand pushed the box back and closed the closet door. Then she crawled under her bed to get the disk she had hidden there. She knelt beside her bed opened her hand and looked at the disks she had made. Now they looked ugly and stupid to her. They weren't perfect circles like the moon. The disks were her one chance to get those moments right, to describe them so she could remember, and she hadn't be able to do it.

Christine got a big spoon from the drawer in the kitchen and went outside in her bare feet and her housecoat and the rags in her hair. The door banged behind her and the grass was cold and damp under her feet as she ran to tree in the backyard. Her mother shouted at her.

– Christine! What are you doing? Get back in the house! What are you doing?

The dog next door ran to the fence and barked at her. The eyes of the street lights shone down on Christine as she dug a hole at the root of the tree and put the disks into it. The smell of the night air and the damp earth and the dark and the eclipse. She covered the disks with the dirt and ran back into the house.

The moon began to reappear.

## acknowledgements

John, thank you for your unwavering support.

Thanks to Tom Wharton whose insight and comments helped shape this book.

Doug Barbour, Natalie Olsen, Matt Bowes, Paul Matwychuk — Edmonton's Santa Rosa neighbourhood lives on thanks to NeWest Press.

I would also like to acknowledge the music and films that play behind *North East:*

> *Cleopatra,* Dir. Joseph L. Mankiewicz, Perf. Elizabeth Taylor, Richard Burton, Rex Harrison, 20th Century Fox, 1963.

*Father of the Bride,* Dir. Vincente Minnelli, Perf. Spencer Tracy, Elizabeth Taylor, Joan Bennett, Metro-Goldwyn-Mayer, 1950.

Gummoe, John Claude, "Rhythm of the Falling Rain" (performed by The Cascades). Valiant Records, 1962.

Hatch, Tony, "Downtown" (performed by Petula Clark). Warner Bros, 1964.

Lipton, Leonard and Peter Yarrow, "Puff the Magic Dragon" (performed by Peter, Paul and Mary). Warner Bros/WEA. Recorded 1962. Released 1963.

Pomus, Jerome "Doc" and Mort Shuman, "Can't Get Used to Losing You" (performed by Andy Williams). Columbia Records, 1963.

Wayne, Bernie and Lee Morris, "Blue Velvet" (performed by Bobby Vinton). Epic Records, 1963.

Wendy McGrath was born in Prince Albert, Saskatchewan and now lives in Edmonton. Her poetry and short fiction have been published in *Descant, Prairie Fire,* and *Grain. Santa Rosa,* her second novel, was released by NeWest Press in 2011.

¶ This book was typeset in Dante MT, which was designed by Giovanni Mardersteig in 1954.